My Day with Anka

By Nan Ferring Nelson
Illustrated by Bill Farnsworth

Lothrop, Lee & Shepard Books   New York

*T*o my family, especially my brothers Mike and Tom—BOO!

And in loving memory of Anna Dlask
NFN

*T*o Caitlin
BF

Text copyright © 1996 by Nan Ferring Nelson
Illustrations copyright © 1996 by Bill Farnsworth
All rights reserved. No part of this book may be reproduced or utilized in any form or by any means, electronic or mechanical,
including photocopying and recording, or by any information storage and retrieval system,
without permission in writing from the Publisher. Inquiries should be addressed to Lothrop, Lee & Shepard Books,
a division of William Morrow & Company, Inc., 1350 Avenue of the Americas, New York, New York 10019.
Printed in the United States of America
First Edition   1 2 3 4 5 6 7 8 9 10
Library of Congress Cataloging in Publication Data
Nelson, Nan Ferring.
My day with Anka / by Nan Ferring Nelson; illustrated by Bill Farnsworth.
p.   cm.   Summary: When Anka comes each week on Thursday,
young Karrie enjoys her Czech cooking and helps her with the housework.
ISBN 0-688-11058-4. — ISBN 0-688-11059-2 (lib. bdg.)
[1. Immigrants—Fiction. 2. Home economics—Fiction. 3. Friendship—Fiction.] I. Farnsworth, Bill, ill. II. Title.
PZ7.N43575My 1996 [Fic]—dc20 95-25425 CIP AC

The illustrations in this book were done in acrylic paints on canvas. The display type was set in Goudy Handtooled.
The text was set in Horley Old Style. Color separations by Colotone Graphics. Printed and bound by Worzallla Graphics.
Production supervision by Bonnie King. Designed by Charlotte Hommey.

On Thursday mornings Karrie smells the warm rolls before she even opens her eyes. Quick, quick, she tumbles out of bed, pulling Rabbit behind her by one ear. "It's Anka's day," she tells him. "Kolaches for breakfast!"

"Shh," she whispers as she tiptoes down the hall past Mommy and Daddy's closed door, then softly, softly down the stairs, making sure she skips the squeaky step. Pressing her back to the dining room wall, she inches her way to the kitchen door and peeks around it.

There is Anka, ironing Daddy's shirts. *P-s-s-h, p-s-s-h* the iron hisses on the collar. The bow on Anka's apron jiggles as she works. She whisks the shirt off the board and sets the iron down. This is the moment Karrie has been waiting for.

"BOO!"

Anka jumps, then laughs. "I get you, you rascal!"
She reaches for Karrie but misses. "I get you now, my
little Karichka." Anka kicks off her shoes. Daddy's
shirt is a ghost flying over her head. Her feet pound the
floor, and it shakes when she changes directions. "I get
you easy. I go the other way." Karrie darts ahead of
Anka's zigzags. Then Anka backs up and twists the
skirt of her dress into pants. "Here I come. I jump over
the top!"

Karrie scoots under the table and pops up right in
her own chair. "I win, I win!" she cries.

"I think I get the heart attack. Too old for such games. Too big to fit under tables." Anka wraps Karrie up in a good-morning hug. "Now eat the breakfast, Karichka."

Mmmm. Kolaches. Karrie licks the sugar off the top before she bites into the fruit. Today it's apricot—Karrie's favorite. "Do I smell kolaches?" asks Mommy from the doorway.

"And Anka's coffee," says Daddy. They love Anka's breakfasts, too—so much, it makes them late.

Finally Anka points to the clock. "Eight o'clock," she tells them. "Go! Everybody do the work, now."

Anka buttons Karrie's sweater up to her chin and ties a scarf around her head.

"Such a pretty face in the babushka," she says as she ties the knot.

Anka has a pretty face, too, with pink, wrinkly cheeks and small spaces between her teeth that make her smile as jolly as a jack-o'-lantern's.

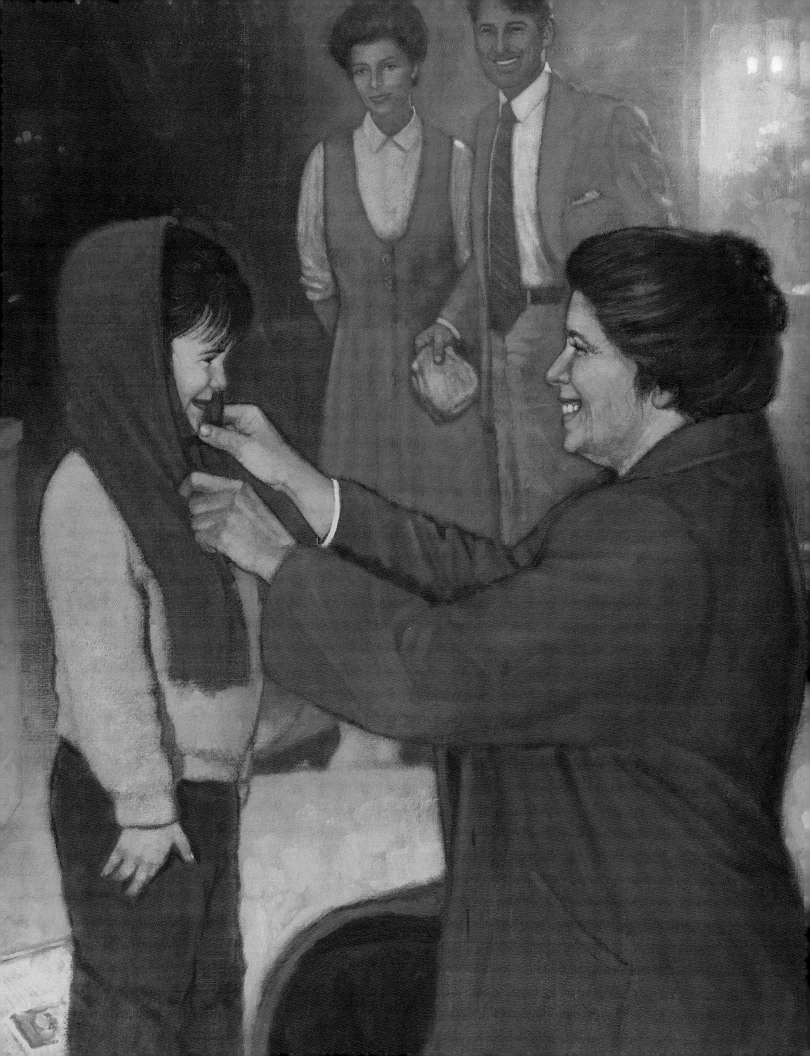

Anka pours stinky ammonia into hot water in a bucket. "Here, you carry these," she says, handing Karrie a stack of old newspapers. "They make good window rags, ya? Come, we let in the good light!"

Outside, they prop the ladder against the house. Its legs sink into the dirt like stems among the sunflowers. Anka climbs to the top to be the blossom, and Karrie is the root, holding the ladder steady so Anka won't fall.

Anka washes a window, then crumples a newspaper and makes giant circles on the glass. S-q-u-e-a-k, s-q-u-e-a-k. "Squeaky clean!" she announces. She climbs down her stem, and they plant her farther along in the garden under the bedroom windows. When they have worked all the way around to the back door again, Anka throws the dirty water onto the driveway.

"See here, Karichka, the Atlantic Ocean. I stand in the Old Country and you stand across. Ya, there now, you're beside the Statue of Liberty," says Anka. "One time I ride a big boat. The waves go everywhere. The boat is up and down, up and down, and a little bit straight ahead."

"Did you have kolaches?" asks Karrie.

"Oh, ya, ya. But the soup, it spills every day. I get hungry when I think of it!"

"Me, too!" says Karrie. She puts both feet together and jumps, *splat,* into the Atlantic Ocean. Anka does the same. Then they make wet footprints up the steps and take off their shoes at the kitchen door.

Anka takes the leftovers out of the refrigerator for lunch. She lines up the meat and potatoes and vegetables on the counter. Then she stuffs them all into the food grinder. Karrie helps.

"Worms are coming out!" Karrie shouts. "We're having worms for lunch."

"You don't like my food, you rascal! You make me cry," says Anka. Tears roll down her face, but her shoulders bounce up and down like laughing.

"Those are onion tears, you rascal," says Karrie. Her eyes pinch and water, too.

Anka dabs Karrie's cheeks with the corner of a towel. "Skunks and onions," she says. "They make us cry."

Karrie and Anka squeeze the hash into patties that sizzle when they hit the pan. Anka cuts the brown spots off peaches and plums and bakes them for dessert. "Eating the hash makes strong bones," she says.

"And shiny hair, like mine," says Karrie between spoonfuls.

After lunch Anka dusts Karrie's room while Karrie stacks her favorite books beside her bed. "I'm reading all these for quiet time," she says. She wraps her quilt around herself and Rabbit and props a book on her knees.

"You read me books someday, too, my Karichka," says Anka. Then she softly closes the door.

"Toot-toot! All aboard. This way, the train to Prague!" calls Anka. Quiet time is over. Karrie runs into the living room and helps Anka push the armchairs into a row behind the footstools and the piano bench. Rabbit is the engineer.

"All aboard!" says Karrie. She takes tickets and helps the passengers with their bags.

"Chug-chug-chug-chug, CHUG-chug-chug-chug," says Anka, as she vacuums the tracks ahead. "Tell the people, look out the windows. They hear a song, 'Anka Goes to the Cabbage Patch.'" She sings, *"Shla Anka do zeli, do zeli, do zeli."*

Karrie points to Anka. "See the one with the flowers in her hair?" she tells the passengers. "She's never had a haircut in her whole life. Right, Anka?"

"Oh, ya, ya, that's so." Anka touches her hair and pushes in the pins that have come loose. Karrie loves the braids that go around and around Anka's head. They don't seem to start anywhere or ever end.

The train chugs into the countryside, "TOOT-TOOT!" and Anka vacuums the railroad station.

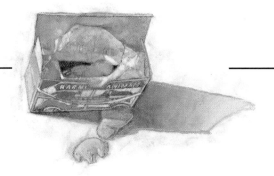

When Mommy comes home, the whole house is sparkling. Karrie races to hold the door for her as she brings in the groceries.

"Did you buy animal crackers?" asks Karrie.

"They're right on top," says Mommy.

At five o'clock, right on the dot, they hear a honk outside.

"My Kuba, he's always on time," says Anka. She puts on her coat and ties her babushka, then picks up the coffee can of bacon grease that Mommy has saved. "I make soap for my Kuba," she says.

"Ick! From that?" says Karrie.

Anka catches her in a great big hug. "My little Karichka!" Karrie nestles into her arms and her warm smell.

Kuba tips his hat to Karrie before he backs the old blue car down the driveway. Anka turns in her seat to blow kisses. "Next week we make noodles," she shouts. "Yippee!" Karrie waves her hand as hard as she can. "Good-bye, my Anka. Good-bye!"